The Elves
and the
Shoemaker

Retold by Jenny Giles

Illustrated by Sue O'Loughlin

NELSON PRICE MILBURN

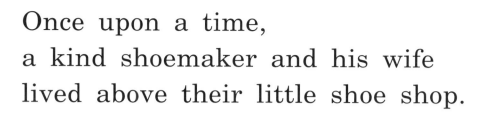

Once upon a time,
a kind shoemaker and his wife
lived above their little shoe shop.

For many years,
everyone in the town
had come to the shop
to buy shoes.

But now, no one came,
and the shoemaker and his wife
were very poor.

One day,
the shoemaker said to his wife,
"I have just enough leather
to make one last pair of shoes.
I will cut them out tonight
and finish making them
in the morning."

So the shoemaker cut the leather
and left it on the table.
Then he and his wife
went upstairs to bed.

In the morning,
the shoemaker looked down
at the table in surprise.

There stood the most beautiful
pair of shoes that he had
ever seen.

"Look at those tiny stitches!"
said the shoemaker's wife.
"Who could have made
such beautiful shoes?"

"I do not know,"
said the shoemaker,
"but I will try to sell them."

The shoemaker put the shoes
into his shop window,
and they were soon sold.

"You have been paid well!"
said the shoemaker's wife.
"Now we have enough money
to buy leather for two more
pairs of shoes."

That night,
the shoemaker cut the new leather
and left it on the table.

9

The next morning,
when the shoemaker woke up,
he found **two** pairs of shoes
waiting for him.
"We have more shoes to sell today!"
cried his wife.

Every night, the shoemaker
cut out more leather
and left it on the table.

And every morning,
he found more shoes
ready for him to sell.
People came from far and wide
to buy the beautiful shoes.

One day,
the shoemaker's wife said,
"We are very lucky.
We have had so many
pairs of shoes made for us.
But how can we find out
who is doing all the work?"

"We will stay awake tonight,"
said the shoemaker.
"Then we will see who is coming
to help us."

So that night, after the shoemaker
had cut the leather,
he and his wife went upstairs.

They sat,
  and watched,
    and waited...

Then, at midnight,
the shoemaker and his wife
had a great surprise.
They saw two tiny elves
climb in the window
and jump down onto the table.
The elves ran to the leather
and began to stitch.

When they had finished
making the shoes, the elves
disappeared out the window.

The shoemaker's wife said,
"The little elves have made
all those shoes for us!
But what can we do for them?"

"The elves had very ragged clothes,"
said the shoemaker.

"Yes, they did!"
said the shoemaker's wife.
"I could make some new clothes
for them."

So the shoemaker's wife
stitched all day, and by nightfall,
she had made new clothes
for the elves.
The shoemaker found
some soft leather, and he made
two pairs of tiny shoes.

"Let us put the clothes
here on the table
where the elves will see them,"
said the shoemaker's wife.

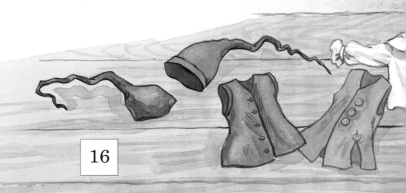

17

Once again,
the shoemaker and his wife
saw the little elves come in
through the window at midnight.

The elves ran to the clothes
and put them on.
They laughed and danced together
on the table.

Then, with a hop and a jump,
they disappeared out the window
and were never seen again.

And the kind shoemaker
and his wife
lived happily ever after,
making beautiful shoes
just as the elves had done.

A play

The Elves and the Shoemaker

People in the play

 Reader

 Shoemaker

 Shoemaker's wife

 Two elves (mime only)

Reader

Once upon a time,
a kind shoemaker and his wife
lived above their little shoe shop.
For many years,
everyone in the town
had come to the shop
to buy shoes.
But now, no one came,
and the shoemaker and his wife
were very poor.

Shoemaker

Wife, I have just enough leather
to make one last pair of shoes.
I will cut them out tonight
and finish making them
in the morning.

Reader

So the shoemaker cut the leather
and left it on the table.
Then he and his wife
went upstairs to bed.

In the morning,
the shoemaker looked down
at the table in surprise.

Shoemaker

Look on the table, Wife!
Someone has made the leather
into a pair of shoes.

Wife

Look at those tiny stitches!
Who could have made
such beautiful shoes?

Shoemaker

I do not know,
but I will try to sell them.

Reader

The shoemaker put the shoes
into his shop window,
and they were soon sold.

Wife

You have been paid well!
Now we have enough money
to buy leather for two more
pairs of shoes.

Shoemaker

I will cut out
the new leather tonight
and leave it on the table.

Reader

The next morning,
when the shoemaker woke up,
he found **two** pairs of shoes
waiting for him.

Wife

We have more shoes to sell today!

Reader

Every night, the shoemaker
cut out more leather
and left it on the table.
And every morning, he found
more shoes ready for him to sell.
People came from far and wide
to buy the beautiful shoes.

Wife

We are very lucky.
We have had so many
pairs of shoes made for us.
But how can we find out
who is doing all the work?

Shoemaker

We will stay awake tonight.
Then we will see
who is coming to help us.

Reader

So that night, after the shoemaker
had cut the leather,
he and his wife went upstairs.
They sat, and watched,
and waited...

Shoemaker

Look, Wife! Two tiny elves
are climbing in the window!

Wife

Could **they** be making the shoes
for us?

Shoemaker

Yes! They must be!
They are stitching the leather!

Reader

When they had finished
making the shoes, the elves
disappeared out the window.

Wife

The little elves have made
all those shoes for us!
But what can we do for them?

Shoemaker

The elves had very ragged clothes.

Wife

Yes, they did!
I could make some new clothes
for them!

Reader

So the shoemaker's wife
stitched all day.

Wife

I have finished making
the new clothes for the elves.

Shoemaker

I have made two pairs
of tiny shoes from soft leather.

Wife

Let us put the clothes
here on the table
where the elves will see them.

Reader

Once again,
the shoemaker and his wife
saw the little elves come in
through the window at midnight.

Reader

The elves ran to the clothes
and put them on.
They laughed and danced together
on the table.
Then, with a hop and a jump,
they disappeared out the window
and were never seen again.

And the kind shoemaker
and his wife
lived happily ever after,
making beautiful shoes
just as the elves had done.